Sailor &
the Balloons

Written by Jill Eggleton
Illustrated by Jim Storey

Rigby

The captain called
the sailors.

"You don't have to
work today," she said.
"But you must keep
the boat going.
I'm staying in bed."

Cool!

What will
we do?

2

The sailors were happy.
They didn't like working
every day.

"What will we do?"
they asked.

"We could have some races,"
said Sailor Sam.
"We could race up
the boat and back again."

4

The sailors ran up the deck.
But they fell over
the ropes and buckets.

"This is no good," they said.
"What can we do now?"

"We could have
a race up the mast,"
said Sailor Sam.

Help!

I'm going
to win!

7

So all the sailors
got on the mast.

But there were too
many sailors, and
the mast went . . .

crack!

The sailors fell
onto the deck.

"Help," they said.
"The boat won't keep
going now.
What can we do?"

Sailor Sam went away.

When he came back,
he had a big bag
of balloons.

"We'll blow up
the balloons," he said.
"We'll tie them to the boat.
The balloons will keep
the boat going."

11

The captain looked
out the window.
She could see that
the boat was going fast
over the water.

"Good," she said.
"I can stay in bed."

So the captain stayed in bed.
The sailors had to fix the mast.
And Sailor Sam had to blow up
balloons **all** day!

Guide Notes

Title: Sailor Sam and the Balloons
Stage: Early (4) – Green

Genre: Fiction
Approach: Guided Reading
Processes: Thinking Critically, Exploring Language, Processing Information
Written and Visual Focus: Action/Consequence Chart, Speech Bubbles
Word Count: 215

THINKING CRITICALLY
(sample questions)
- What do you think this story could be about? Look at the title and discuss.
- Where do you think this story takes place?
- Look at pages 2 and 3. Why do you think the captain has given the sailors the day off?
- Look at pages 4 and 5. Why do you think the sailors didn't like working every day?
- Look at pages 6 and 7. What do you think the sailors could do with the buckets and ropes so they didn't fall over them?
- Look at pages 10 and 11. What else do you think the sailors could use to help keep the boat going?
- Look at page 14. Why do you think Sailor Sam has to keep blowing up balloons?

EXPLORING LANGUAGE

Terminology
Title, cover, illustrations, author, illustrator

Vocabulary
Interest words: sailor, races, balloons, ropes, buckets, mast
High-frequency words: called, must, keep, could, won't
Positional words: up, in, over, on, onto, out

Print Conventions
Capital letter for sentence beginnings and names (**S**ailor **S**am), periods, commas, exclamation marks, quotation marks, question marks, ellipsis